JE   DEC 0 5 2005
Schoberle, Cecile.
Storm chaser!

LITTLE SIMON
An imprint of Simon & Schuster Children's Publishing Division
1230 Avenue of the Americas, New York, New York 10020
Copyright © 2004 by Mattel, Inc.
MATCHBOX and all associated logos are trademarks owned by
and used under license from Mattel, Inc. All rights reserved.
LITTLE SIMON is a registered trademark of Simon & Schuster, Inc.,
and associated colophon is a trademark of Simon & Schuster, Inc.
All rights reserved, including the right of reproduction in whole or in part in any form.
Manufactured in the United States of America.
First Edition
2 4 6 8 10 9 7 5 3 1
Cataloging-in-Publication Data for this book
is available from the Library of Congress.
ISBN 0-689-87338-7

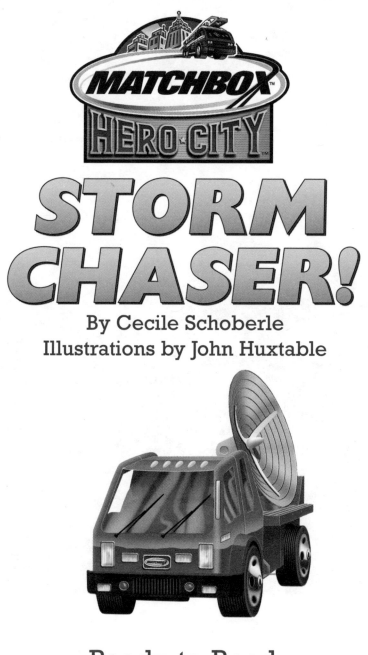

MATCHBOX™

HERO·CITY™

STORM CHASER!

By Cecile Schoberle
Illustrations by John Huxtable

Ready-to-Read

Little Simon

New York London Toronto Sydney

A storm is brewing.

But how do we know

which way

the wind will blow?

Thunder rumbles
and lightning darts.
The radar truck
is ready to start.

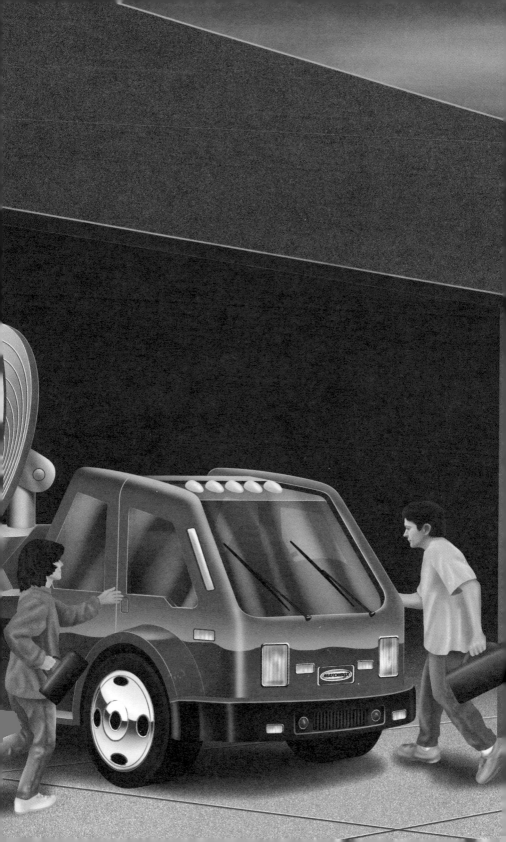

Quick! Jump in!

Follow that storm!

This truck keeps people

free from harm.

The radar turns.

The horn beep-beeps.

Through the rain

the truck slowly creeps.

A twister spins!

The school is called.

The kids go safely

into the halls.

Look! The funnel is
touching down.

It whirls and blows
right through town.

The people are ready.

They know what to do.

The weather truck gave them
plenty of clues.

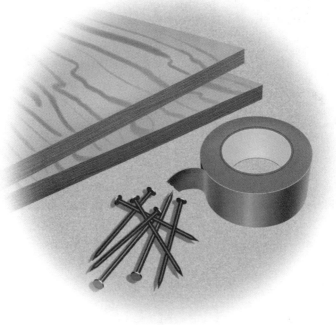

The satellite dish
turns to the sky.
It tracks the clouds
that are passing by.

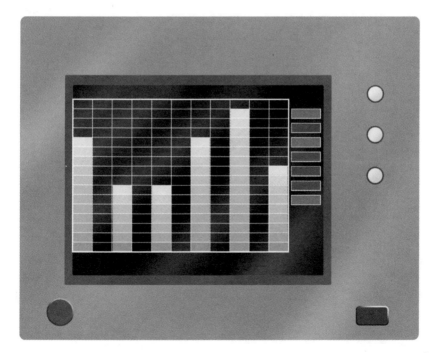

Swish-swash go the wipers.

Blink-blink go the lights.

On and on the truck

drives all night.

When lightning zigzags,
it is time to watch out.

If the sky grows dark,

it is time to get out.

A hurricane swells
and thunders and roars.

It makes big waves
and heads toward shore.

But all the people
are far away.
The weather truck
has saved them today.

Predicting weather
takes more than luck.

We need that great

storm-chaser truck.